Chevrotains

Ruby Daniels

Big Buddy Books
An Imprint of Abdo Publishing
abdobooks.com

abdobooks.com

Published by Abdo Publishing, a division of ABDO, PO Box 398166, Minneapolis, Minnesota 55439.

Printed in the United States of America, North Mankato, Minnesota
102024
012025

Design: Elena Klinkner, Mighty Media, Inc.
Production: Mighty Media, Inc.
Editor: Liz Salzmann
Cover Photograph: teekayu/Shutterstock
Interior Photographs: Christina/Adobe Stock, p. 5; Danny Ye/Adobe Stock, p. 23 (building); Ho VanTri/Shutterstock, p. 17 (top); Hongqilim/Wikimedia Commons, p. 23 (coat of arms); kajornyot/Adobe Stock, p. 7; Michal Sloviak/Shutterstock, p. 27; Miroslav/Adobe Stock, p. 29; NikkiHoff/Shutterstock, p. 16 (top); Plutonian_p/Shutterstock, p. 9; Ranil. susantha/Shutterstock, p. 17 (bottom); Sangur/Adobe Stock, p. 19; stas111/Adobe Stock, p. 20 (compass rose); Supravee Phathunyupong/Shutterstock, p. 11; tanarch/Adobe Stock, pp. 20–21 (maps); Try_my_best/Shutterstock, pp. 13, 25; YAMASA/Shutterstock, p. 15
Design Elements: flovie/Shutterstock Images (patchwork pattern); Mighty Media, Inc. (series logos & icons)

Library of Congress Control Number: 2024938318

Publisher's Cataloging-in-Publication Data
Names: Daniels, Ruby, author.
Title: Chevrotains / by Ruby Daniels
Description: Minneapolis, Minnesota : ABDO Publishing, 2025 | Series: Odd but adorable animals | Includes online resources and index.
Identifiers: ISBN 9781098295127 (lib. bdg.) | ISBN 9798384915171 (ebook)
Subjects: LCSH: Chevrotains--Juvenile literature. | Mouse-deer--Juvenile literature. | Herbivores--Juvenile literature. | Rain forest animals--Juvenile literature. | Hoofed animals--Juvenile literature. | Curiosities and wonders--Juvenile literature.
Classification: DDC 599.65--dc23

Contents

A Chevrotain Encounter

While exploring a forest in Thailand, you hear a rustle near the trail. You turn your head and see a tiny reddish-brown creature eating leaves. It looks like a deer with its hoofed, skinny legs and short tail. But it's barely taller than a cat. You've just spotted the odd but adorable chevrotain!

Chevrotains are also known as mouse deer.

A Closer Look

Chevrotains look like tiny deer with mouselike faces. But chevrotains aren't deer or mice. They belong to their own family of ten different chevrotain **species**. Chevrotains are **ungulates**, or animals with four hooves. They can weigh anywhere from 3 to 35 pounds (1.3 to 16 kg). They can stand 10 to 16 inches (25 to 40 cm) tall.

Chevrotains have white underbellies. Some also have coats with white stripes or spots.

Life as a Chevrotain

Different **species** of chevrotain are active at different times of day or night. They are very shy and mostly live on their own. Female chevrotains can have babies year-round. Baby chevrotains can walk within an hour of birth. They stay hidden, and their mothers return to feed them.

A chevrotain establishes a home territory about as big as five city blocks.

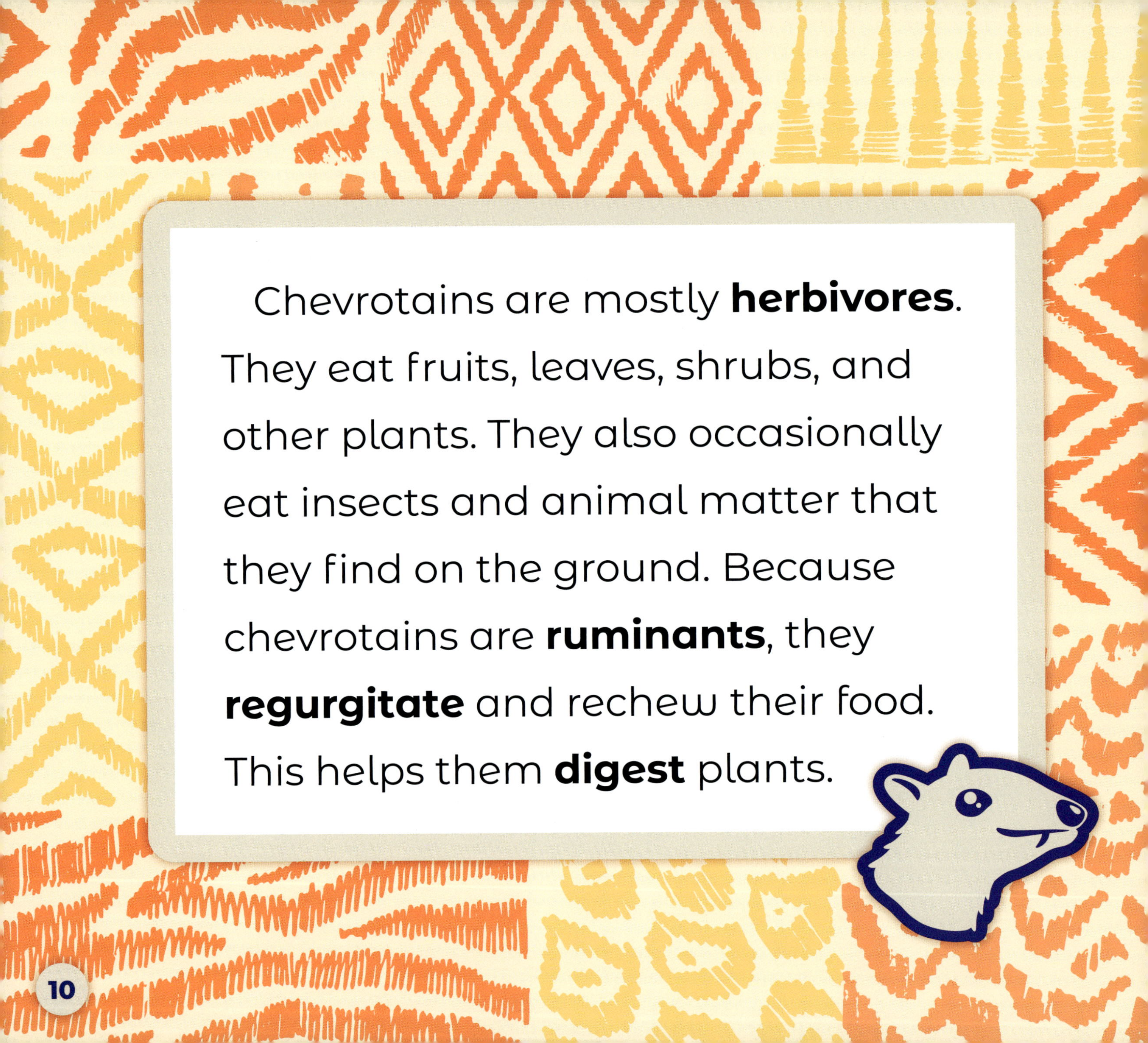

Chevrotains are mostly **herbivores**. They eat fruits, leaves, shrubs, and other plants. They also occasionally eat insects and animal matter that they find on the ground. Because chevrotains are **ruminants**, they **regurgitate** and rechew their food. This helps them **digest** plants.

Because chevrotains are small, they don't eat very much. So, they can take time to find food that is easy for them to digest.

Unique Ungulates

Chevrotains are special in many ways. They are the smallest hoofed **mammals** in the world. And they are the only **ungulates** that have fangs. Some **species** of chevrotain can swim. The water chevrotain can stay underwater for four minutes.

Male chevrotains have longer fangs than females. Males use them to fight one another.

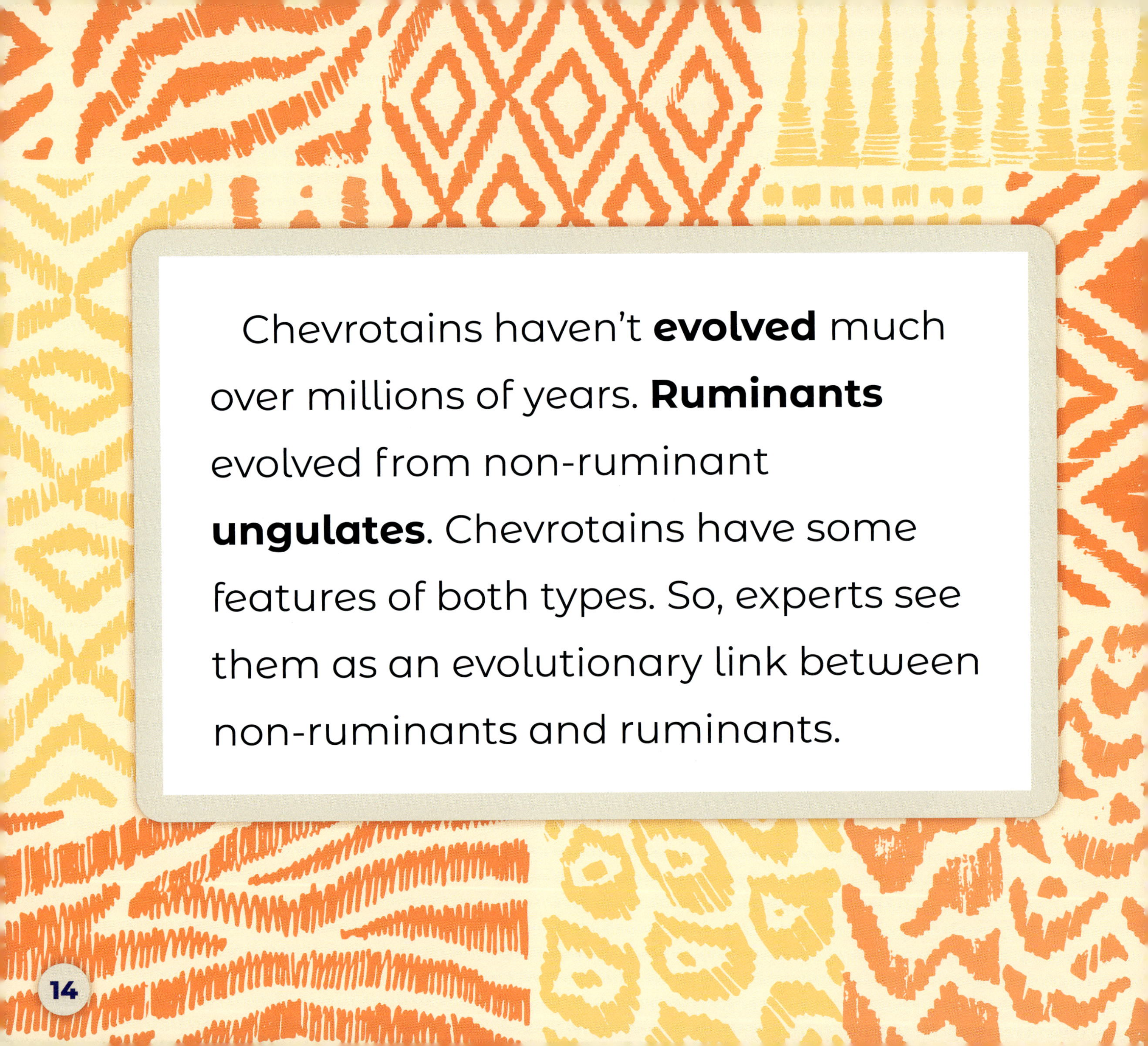

Chevrotains haven't **evolved** much over millions of years. **Ruminants** evolved from non-ruminant **ungulates**. Chevrotains have some features of both types. So, experts see them as an evolutionary link between non-ruminants and ruminants.

Chevrotains are sometimes called "living fossils" because of how little they've evolved.

Creature Feature

The word *chevrotain* comes from the French word for "goat."

Female chevrotains give birth two or three times each year. They usually have one baby at a time.

Most **ruminants** have two toes. But chevrotains have four toes, like pigs.

Chevrotain mothers stand with one hind leg raised when feeding their young.

Species with spots or stripes are called chevrotains. Species without spots or stripes are called mouse deer.

Happy Homes

Most **species** of chevrotain live in South and Southeast Asia. But the water chevrotain lives in West and Central Africa. All species live in **tropical** forests. They often hide from predators under plants on the forest floor. Chevrotains tend to live near water, especially the water chevrotain.

Animals that hunt chevrotains include leopards (*pictured*), crocodiles, and eagles.

Location Station

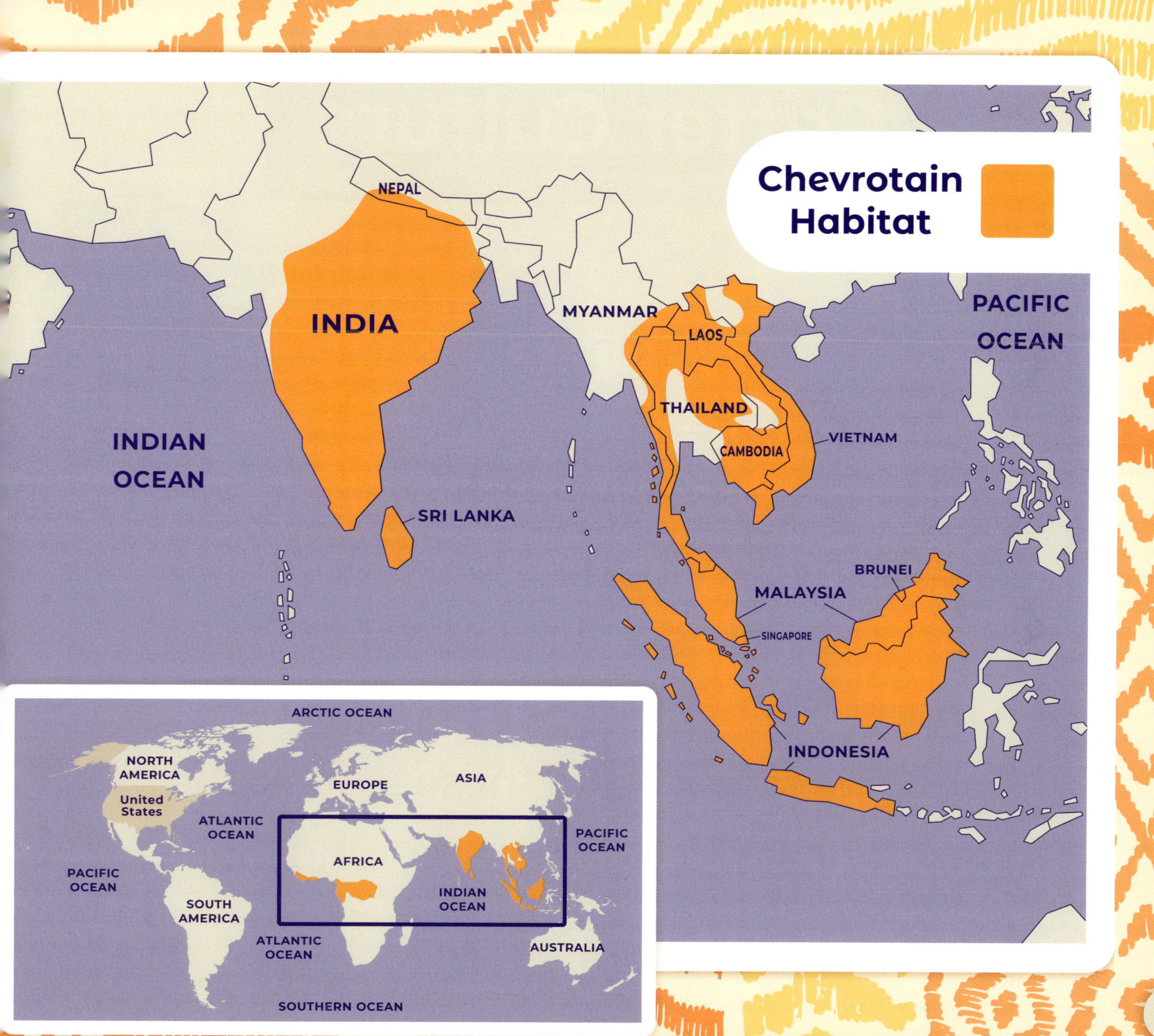
Chevrotain Habitat
NEPAL
INDIA
MYANMAR
LAOS
THAILAND
CAMBODIA
VIETNAM
PACIFIC OCEAN
INDIAN OCEAN
SRI LANKA
BRUNEI
MALAYSIA
SINGAPORE
INDONESIA
ARCTIC OCEAN
NORTH AMERICA
United States
EUROPE
ASIA
ATLANTIC OCEAN
AFRICA
PACIFIC OCEAN
PACIFIC OCEAN
INDIAN OCEAN
SOUTH AMERICA
ATLANTIC OCEAN
AUSTRALIA
SOUTHERN OCEAN

Critter Culture

Chevrotains are an important part of some **cultures** where they live. Malacca is a region of Malaysia. It is spelled Melaka in the Malay language. The chevrotain is a main character in many Malay, Indonesian, and Philippine folktales. In these stories, the chevrotain is often a trickster who fools predators such as crocodiles.

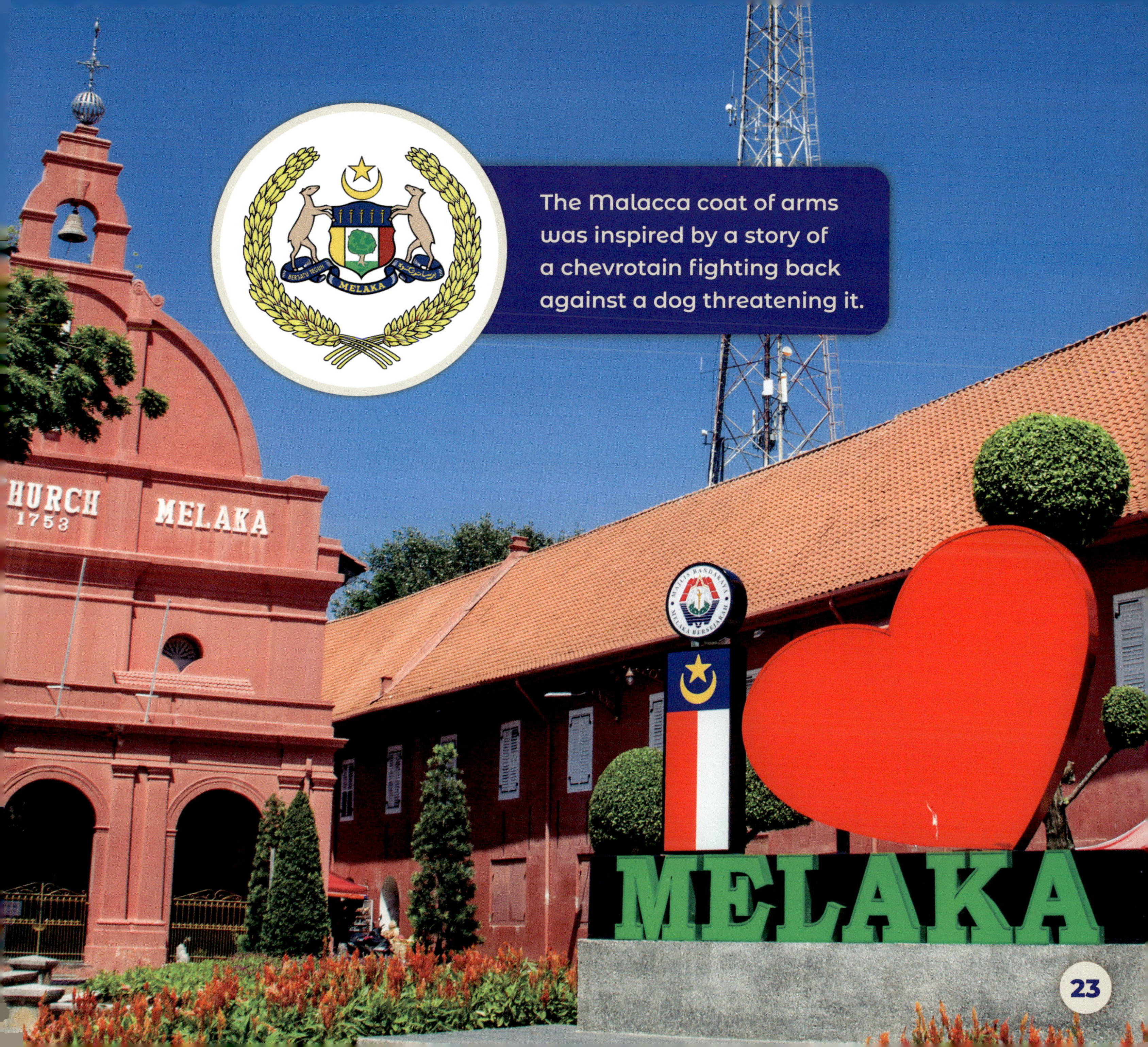

The Malacca coat of arms was inspired by a story of a chevrotain fighting back against a dog threatening it.

Amazing Investigations

Chevrotains are difficult to study because they are hard to find. One **species**, the silver-backed chevrotain, was photographed for the first time ever in 2019! Scientists study chevrotain behaviors, how their bodies relate to **evolution**, and their sleep patterns.

Information that researchers gather can help conservation groups learn how to protect chevrotains from becoming endangered.

Threats and Hope

Most **species** of chevrotain are not **endangered**. However, their populations are decreasing. The main **threats** to chevrotains are hunting by humans and **habitat** loss. Organizations are working to increase zoo breeding programs and improve **enforcement** of hunting laws.

There are laws against hunting chevrotains in many areas. But some hunters set up snares to trap them illegally.

Odd or Adorable?

Chevrotains are unusual and beloved animals. They look strange, but they're also considered cute by many people around the world. What do you think makes an animal odd? What makes an animal adorable? Do you think chevrotains are odd, adorable, or both? Why?

A chevrotain's small size helps it move through thick jungle plants.

Glossary

culture (KUHL-chuhr)—the arts, beliefs, and ways of life of a group of people.

digest (dye-JEHST)—to break down food into parts small enough for the body to use.

endangered—having few left in the world.

enforcement (ihn-FAWR-smuhnt)—the act of carrying out something, such as laws.

evolve—to change or develop slowly over time. Something related to evolving is evolutionary. The process of evolving is evolution.

habitat—a place where a living thing is naturally found.

herbivore (HUHR-buh-vawr)—an animal that eats plants.

mammal—an animal that makes milk to feed its babies and usually has hair or fur on its skin.

regurgitate (ree-GUHR-juh-tayt)—to bring back up from the stomach.

ruminant—an animal that chews its cud. A ruminant's stomach has three or four parts.

species (SPEE-sheez)—living things that are very much alike.

threat—something that could be harmful.

tropical—in a part of the world where temperatures are warm and the air is moist all the time.

ungulate—a plant-eating animal with four hooves. Ungulates include cows, deer, pigs, and horses.

Online Resources

To learn more about chevrotains, please visit **abdobooklinks.com** or scan this QR code. These links are routinely monitored and updated to provide the most current information available.

Index